THE TALE OF
JOHNNY TOWN-MOUSE

BY BEATRIX POTTER

FREDERICK WARNE

TO AESOP IN THE SHADOWS

FREDERICK WARNE

Published by the Penguin Group
Registered office: 80 Strand, London, WC2R 0RL
Penguin Young Readers Group, 345 Hudson Street, New York, N.Y. 10014, USA

First published 1918 by Frederick Warne
This edition with new reproductions of Beatrix Potter's book illustrations first published 2007
This edition copyright © Frederick Warne & Co. 2007
Reissued 2016
New reproductions of Beatrix Potter's book illustrations copyright © Frederick Warne & Co. 2002
Original copyright in text and illustrations © Frederick Warne & Co., 1918

Manufactured in China

Special Markets ISBN 978-0-241-29831-2

JOHNNY TOWN-MOUSE was born in a
cupboard. Timmy Willie was born in a garden.
Timmy Willie was a little country mouse who
went to town by mistake in a hamper. The
gardener sent vegetables to town once a week by
carrier; he packed them in a big hamper.

The gardener left the hamper by the garden gate,
so that the carrier could pick it up when he passed.
Timmy Willie crept in
through a hole in
the wickerwork,
and after eating
some peas –
Timmy Willie fell
fast asleep.

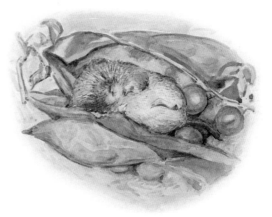

HE awoke in a fright, while the hamper was
being lifted into the carrier's cart. Then there was
a jolting, and a clattering of horse's feet; other
packages were thrown in; for miles and miles
— jolt — jolt — jolt! and Timmy Willie trembled
amongst the jumbled up vegetables.

AT last the cart stopped at a house, where the hamper was taken out, carried in, and set down. The cook gave the carrier sixpence; the back door banged, and the cart rumbled away. But there was no quiet; there seemed to be hundreds of carts

passing. Dogs barked; boys whistled in the street; the cook laughed, the parlour maid ran up and down stairs; and a canary sang like a steam engine.

TIMMY WILLIE, who had lived all his life in a garden, was almost frightened to death. Presently the cook opened the hamper and began to unpack the vegetables. Out sprang the terrified Timmy Willie.

Up jumped the cook on a chair, exclaiming "A mouse! a mouse! Call the cat! Fetch me the poker, Sarah!" Timmy Willie did not wait for Sarah with the poker; he rushed along the skirting-board till he came to a little hole, and in he popped.

10

HE dropped half a foot, and crashed into the middle of a mouse dinner party, breaking three glasses. —"Who in the world is this?" inquired Johnny Town-mouse. But after the first exclamation of surprise he instantly recovered his manners.

WITH the utmost politeness he introduced
Timmy Willie to nine other mice, all with long
tails and white neckties. Timmy Willie's own tail
was insignificant. Johnny Town-mouse and his
friends noticed it; but they were too well bred to
make personal remarks; only one of them asked
Timmy Willie if he had ever been in a trap?

THE dinner was of eight courses; not much of
anything, but truly elegant. All the dishes were
unknown to Timmy Willie, who would have been
a little afraid of tasting them; only he was very
hungry, and very anxious to behave with company
manners. The continual noise upstairs made him
so nervous, that he dropped a plate. "Never mind,
they don't belong to us," said Johnny.

"WHY don't those youngsters come back with the dessert?" It should be explained that two young mice, who were waiting on the others, went skirmishing upstairs to the kitchen between courses. Several times they had come tumbling in, squeaking and laughing; Timmy Willie learnt with horror that they were being chased by the cat. His appetite failed, he felt faint.

"Try some jelly?" said Johnny Town-mouse.

"No? Would you rather go to bed? I will show you a most comfortable sofa pillow."

The sofa pillow had a hole in it. Johnny Town-mouse quite honestly recommended it as the best bed, kept exclusively for visitors.

BUT the sofa smelt of cat. Timmy Willie preferred to spend a miserable night under the fender.

It was just the same next day. An excellent breakfast was provided — for mice accustomed to eat bacon; but

Timmy Willie had been reared on roots and salad. Johnny Town-mouse and his friends racketted about under the floors, and came boldly out all over the house in the evening. One particularly loud crash had been caused by Sarah tumbling downstairs with the tea-tray; there were crumbs and sugar and smears of jam to be collected, in spite of the cat.

TIMMY WILLIE longed to be at home in his peaceful nest in a sunny bank. The food disagreed with him; the noise prevented him from sleeping. In a few days he grew so thin that Johnny Town-mouse noticed it, and questioned him. He listened to Timmy Willie's story and inquired about the garden. "It sounds rather a dull place? What do you do when it rains?"

"When it rains, I sit in my little sandy burrow and shell corn and seeds from my Autumn store.

"I peep out at the throstles and blackbirds on the lawn, and my friend Cock Robin. And when the sun comes out again, you should see my garden and the flowers — roses and pinks and pansies — no noise except the birds and bees, and the lambs in the meadows."

"THERE goes that cat again!" exclaimed Johnny Town-mouse. When they had taken refuge in the coal-cellar he resumed the conversation; "I confess I am a little disappointed; we have endeavoured to entertain you, Timothy William."

"Oh yes, yes, you have been most kind; but I do feel so ill," said Timmy Willie.

"IT may be that your teeth and digestion are unaccustomed to our food; perhaps it might be wiser for you to return in the hamper."

"Oh? Oh!" cried Timmy Willie.

"Why of course for the matter of that we could have sent you back last week," said Johnny rather huffily — "did you not know that the hamper goes back empty on Saturdays?"

SO Timmy Willie said goodbye to his new friends, and hid in the hamper with a crumb of cake and a withered cabbage leaf; and after much jolting, he was set down safely in his own garden.

SOMETIMES on Saturdays he went to look at the hamper lying by the gate, but he knew better than to get in again. And nobody got out, though Johnny Town-mouse had half promised a visit.

THE winter passed; the sun came out again;
Timmy Willie sat by his burrow warming his
little fur coat and sniffing the smell of violets
and spring grass.

HE had nearly forgotten his visit to town. When
up the sandy path all spick and span with a brown
leather bag came Johnny Town-mouse!

Timmy Willie received him with open arms.
"You have come at the best of all the year, we will
have herb pudding and sit in the sun."

"H'm'm! it is a little damp," said Johnny Town-
mouse, who was carrying his tail under his arm,
out of the mud.

"WHAT is that fearful noise?" he started violently.

"That?" said Timmy Willie, "that is only a cow; I will beg a little milk, they are quite harmless, unless they happen to lie down upon you. How are all our friends?"

JOHNNY'S account was rather middling. He explained why he was paying his visit so early in the season; the family had gone to the sea-side for Easter; the cook was doing

spring cleaning, on board wages, with particular instructions to clear out the mice. There were four kittens, and the cat had killed the canary.

"THEY say we did it; but I know better,"
said Johnny Town-mouse. "Whatever is that
fearful racket?"

"That is only the lawnmower; I will fetch some
of the grass clippings presently to make your bed.
I am sure you had better settle in the country,
Johnny."

"H'm'm — we shall see by Tuesday week; the
hamper is stopped while they are at the sea-side."

"I am sure you will never want to live in
town again," said Timmy Willie.

BUT he did. He went back in the very next
hamper of vegetables; he said it was too quiet!!

ONE place suits one person, another place suits another person. For my part, I prefer to live in the country, like Timmy Willie.